HEROIN

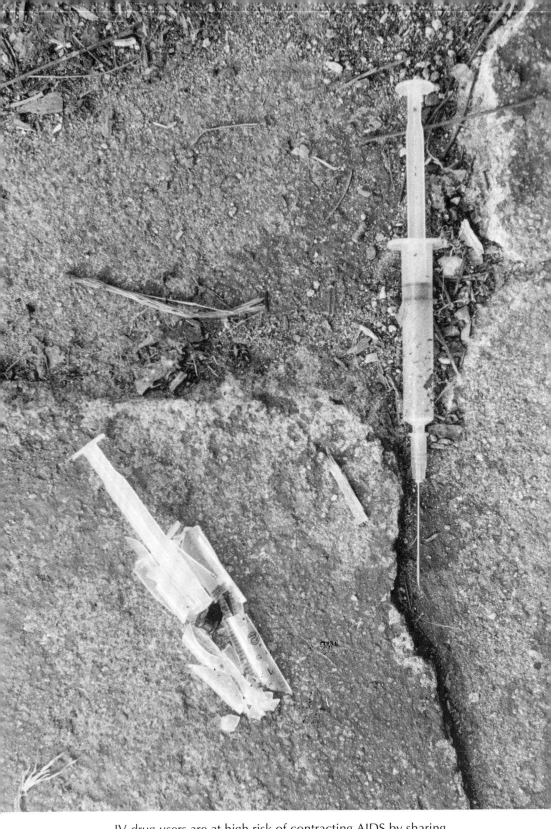

IV-drug users are at high risk of contracting AIDS by sharing needles.

HEROIN

Sandra Lee Smith

THE ROSEN PUBLISHING GROUP, INC.
NEW YORK

To my brother-in-law, Richard,
whose expertise in the prevention of substance abuse
has been invaluable not only to the writing of this book
but to our community.

*The people pictured in this book are only models; they in no way
practice or endorse the activities illustrated. Captions serve only to
explain the subjects of photographs and do not in any way imply a
connection between the real-life models and the staged situations.*

Published in 1991, 1993, 1995 by The Rosen Publishing Group, Inc.
29 East 21st Street, New York, NY 10010

Revised Edition, 1995

Copyright © 1991, 1993, 1995 by the Rosen Publishing Group, Inc.

Printed in Canada.

Library of Congress Cataloging-in-Publication Data

Smith, Sandra Lee
      Heroin / by Sandra Lee Smith
      (The Drug Abuse Prevention Library)
      Includes bibliographical references and index
      Summary: Discusses heroin, its unique qualities and
      dangers, and counsels against illegal involvement with
      the drug.
            ISBN 0-8239-2124-7
            1. Heroin—Juvenile literature. 2. Heroin
            habit—Juvenile literature. [1. Heroin. 2. Drug
            abuse.]
            I. Title II. Series
            HV5809.5S65 1991
            362.29'3—dc20
                                                            91-10676
                                                               CIP
                                                               AC

Contents

Introduction

Heroin, once known as the "heroic" drug, is one of the most addictive and destructive drugs available to teens today.

"I'm bored." Michael stretched out his long legs and shook back a lock of blond hair.

"Yeah," Jason agreed. "School sucks."

"Let's cut out of here."

"And go where?" Jason frowned, his dark brown skin crinkling around his eyes. "Ever since we quit smoking dope, life's been a drag."

Michael sighed. "What I wouldn't give for a joint right now!"

"I know. Where can we get one?"

Jason nodded toward a group of girls standing on the other side of the quad. "Maria has a stash in her locker."

"No kidding?" Michael straightened, paused for a minute, then sank back down. "We can't smoke now. If we get busted we'll be expelled for good."

Jason stood. "We can't get busted for asking."

"Cool it, Bro. I don't want to smoke, I just want to get high." Michael groaned as he watched his friend approach Maria. He half wanted him to come back; then again, if he scored...

Jason returned a few minutes later with Maria. Michael's interest perked up for the first time in days.

"I hear you wanna lift with no smoke." Maria smiled. "I've got just the thing."

Michael stood when he saw the foil in Maria's hand.

"A little Mexican tar, *hombre*."

Juan dropped the tray as the man brushed by. "Did you see him?" Juan barely noticed the tray Leo put back in his hand. "Wasn't that Shawn Clark?"

Leo cast Juan a wry glance. "You working with half a deck these days? Shawn Clark wouldn't be in a place like this." He

8 | gestured at the crowded room where he and Juan volunteered every Saturday afternoon to help feed the homeless drug addicts who drifted in.

"It was him, I swear," Juan insisted as he began to clear the next row of tables.

"Come off it. Clark was our star quarterback. He's got to be playing for some big-time college team by now."

"I heard U.C.L.A. recruited him," Juan agreed. "Still..."

Just then the man they'd been staring at turned around. Juan and Leo both froze. It was Shawn Clark, but it wasn't the Shawn Clark they had known. The once muscular body was now washed-out skin over bare bones. His eyes were sunken in his lined and haggard face. His hair stood on end, unkempt and dirty.

"He looks like a hundred miles of bad road," Juan gasped.

"That's heroin for you," Leo murmured. "It wastes you."

The baby screamed.

Saralyn shuddered as she glanced at her son's red, puckered face. "Shut up!"

The baby continued to wail.

"I can't stand it." Saralyn stomped out of the room and slammed the door. Tears

The athlete works hard to develop his body. He chooses not to harm it with drugs.

10 rolled down her cheeks. If only she had some smack. It would calm her nerves.

Her fingers shook as she dialed the phone.

When Duane answered, she began to cry again.

"Saralyn, is that you?"

"Yes." She could barely speak.

"What's wrong?" Duane sounded worried. "You haven't taken anything, have you?"

"No," she managed to reply. "I need some stuff, D. I ache all over. My skin itches."

"Those are the symptoms of withdrawal. You'll get through."

"Can you bring me a candy bar or something?" She didn't want candy, she wanted the real thing. But she'd been craving sweets.

"Sure thing. Hang in there." Duane spoke firmly. "Remember your son. He needs to come off the drugs too."

Remorse coursed through Saralyn. Her son must feel as bad as she did. How was she to know he'd get high when she breast-fed him?

"It's okay, D. I'll make it." Saralyn hung up the phone and took a deep breath. Yes, she'd make it. She had to. She didn't want her son to go through the hell she had experienced.

Each of these people has been exposed to the ups and downs of heroin. The thing about heroin is that it always ends in a down.

Humans are miracles of creation. Each one of us is unique and designed to get as much or as little out of life as we want. Free will and self-determination allow us to gain our achievements in our own ways. It is impossible to accomplish anything, however, if we destroy ourselves. Heroin is a chemical that destroys the body and the mind.

Our bodies have enough strength and resilience to temporarily resist what is poisonous. But repeated exposure gradually breaks the system down. Eventually the system just stops working. When that happens, you die.

You are a valuable human being. There is no other being created quite like you, no other person can accomplish what you can. You need your body and mind to be able to work at full strength and capacity. You have your own purpose in life to fulfill, your own goals to achieve. It is your responsibility to see that you keep yourself in good working order.

Poppies are beautiful flowers, but they yield a deadly substance.

CHAPTER 1

What Is Heroin?

*H*eroin is a chemical substance derived from the opium poppy. This beautiful flower grows in hot, dry climates. The pod left after the petals fall contains a white syrup that is collected by poppy growers. When the syrup dries, it hardens into a brown substance we call opium.

From opium, chemists extract many of our common drugs. Some of those drugs are used legally for medicinal purposes. Morphine and codeine are the most common ones. They are widely used by doctors as painkillers.

14   Heroin is also a common derivative, but it is illegal in most countries, including the United States. It is considered so harmful and dangerous that it is not even allowed to be used for medicinal purposes. Mainly that is because it is made from the garbage left over after making morphine.

That was not always the case. During the mid-nineteenth century a famous German chemist made heroin to help morphine addicts come off the drug. Morphine was widely used at the time as a painkiller.

The drug was considered a *heroic* substance. Soldiers from the Civil War up to World War I were given heroin to break them of their addiction to morphine. It was after the turn of the century that doctors began to realize that heroin addiction was far worse than morphine.

Now scientists have developed another chemical to assist the heroin addict. Methadone is used by some drug treatment centers throughout the United States to help heroin addicts withdraw. There is concern, however, that methadone is also addictive. In fact, some studies indicate that it is as addictive as heroin.

Manufacture of Heroin   *15*

It is illegal to grow opium poppies in the United States. Even if we could grow them, a laboratory is needed to process the syrup into the powders sold on the street. Such labs are also illegal.

Most of the international supply of opium comes from poppy farms in two major areas: the Golden Crescent and the Golden Triangle. Poppy farms and factories are illegal in those areas also. But the people are so poor that they risk punishment to grow the flowers.

The Golden Crescent is in the Middle East and includes the countries of Iran, Afghanistan, and Pakistan. The Golden Triangle is in South Asia and includes Laos, Burma, and Thailand. All of these countries are very poor. A farmer can earn 97 percent more money from a crop of poppies than from the same amount of grain.

Most of these countries are engaged in wars. Because of that, police action is focused on warfare, leaving little time and money to fight drug trafficking. Also, these countries need expensive weapons. Drugs are often exchanged for arms.

16   In the western United States heroin is imported from Mexico. *Mexican Brown* is a poorly processed grade of heroin made from poppies grown south of the border. It is of very low quality, but the demand for it is so high that the makers see no need to spend money to process a better quality.

These social and economic conditions make it difficult to control the production of opium poppies. As long as people will buy their product, these poor countries will produce opium.

Transporting opium to the United States is illegal. However, opium slips through customs in many ways. Because of the increased attention of law-enforcement agencies, the drug scene on the streets is changing. Shipments of marijuana, which is strong smelling and bulky, are decreasing while opium and cocaine importation is increasing. The more compact substances are easier to smuggle into the country.

Unfortunately, the demand for all these drugs is high. Dealing them on the black market and on the street involves millions of dollars. The power of that much money makes it very hard to control the various

Drug-sniffing dogs help law-enforcement officers to check
luggage at airports.

18 sellers, dealers, and buyers. From the drug barons to the street dealers to the neighborhood pushers to the users themselves, greed and need rule supply and demand.

Because the market is illegal, it is not regulated. That leaves the business wide open to corruption, danger, and death. From the start of the chain in the Middle East and Southeast Asia, dirty laboratories begin the potential for death.

Buyers never know what purity or dosage they are getting in the packs of powder they buy. No laws control what is added to the substance. So a user faces not only addiction and the ill effects of the drug, but the possibility of overdose or poisoning or both.

Dealing the drugs is also dangerous. Heroin is illegal, so whatever level of the business you are involved in is criminal. Criminal activity not only is immoral but involves the dealer with immoral people. Those people are likely to cheat, steal, lie, and even kill. That happens at all levels, from the baron protecting his turf to the addicts who are so desperate for an injection that they kill for it.

You may think you are safe because **19** friends or family supply your needs. But somewhere in your dealing you will come across a possibly life-threatening situation. It could be the quality of the heroin or the person you deal with.

Other Names for Heroin

The big H	Scag
H	Stuff
Smack	Elephant
Chi	Tiger
Dragon	Nanoo
No. 4	Gear
No. 3	China White
Harry	Black Tar
Junk	Chiva
Scat	Mexican Brown
Horse	Tar
Chinese	Mexican Tar

A heroin addict shoots up—injects heroin to get one of many
fixes in a day.

CHAPTER 2

How Does Heroin Affect You?

*H*eroin is a narcotic. The word narcotic comes from the Greek word *narkosis*, which means benumbed. Physically, heroin numbs the senses.

Physical Effects

Our five senses enable us to survive in our environment. Taste, smell, touch, hearing, and sight feed messages to our brain so that we can react to what is around us. If we don't like what is around us, we have choices. We can change the environment, move to a new location, or ignore what is there. Most of us learn to function within the circumstances.

22   As teenagers it is not always possible to make changes. The choice to ignore is difficult, especially if the environment is depressing, lonely, or ugly. The addict's wish is to escape. Chemical substances deaden the senses and let one ignore the surroundings.

The problem with that form of escape is that whatever makes you want to escape doesn't change. Drugs wear off and there you are, still facing the same problems.

A first-time user of heroin often becomes violently ill, with vomiting and a severe headache. Peers or pushers say it will be better the second time. For some, it isn't. Occasional users often suffer from diarrhea, stomach and muscle cramps, and loss of appetite.

Heroin can be taken several ways. It can be smoked or swallowed, but neither way is very effective. The most common method of taking heroin is injecting it. *Skin-popping* is injecting the drug under the skin, not in a vein. A drug user's body builds up a resistance to almost anything it is given. Heroin is no exception. In order to get a high, a user needs more of it each time. Skin-popping soon becomes ineffective.

The user may then begin *mainlining,* injecting heroin directly into a vein. With frequent injections, veins may collapse. When new veins are used, *tracks* may appear on a *junkie's* body. Sometimes a user misses a vein. This can cause an abscess or develop into blood poisoning.

There are several grades of heroin. Many of them are poor. A user generally filters the heroin into the needle through a piece of cotton or a cigarette filter to get rid of any clumps. This leaves some residue on the cotton or filter. This residue is often diluted and given to a first-time user with the mistaken idea that it won't be a very strong dose. This procedure can be dangerous, especially if unsterilized cotton is used.

If you are allergic to heroin or any opiate, you can become violently ill and even die on the first fix. Heroin that has been made and handled poorly, is not measured, or is mixed with poison can cause overdose or death. There is no way of knowing when or if that will happen.

An overdose can cause heart failure, rapid heartbeat, shortness of breath, and ringing in the ears or head. Some heroin overdoses cause coma, or unconsciousness. That is extremely dangerous, as victims can fall and smother or drown in their own vomit.

Daily use of heroin causes extreme constipation and a loss of appetite. Many addicts suffer from malnutrition for one of two reasons: First, they are not hungry. Second, and more commonly, the constipation becomes so painful that they don't want to eat more food.

Emotional Effects

Most people get to heroin because they have been doing other drugs. As we have suggested, use of chemical substances is a form of escape. It is an emotional reaction to one's life situation. Instead of dealing with life, users choose to escape it.

Another emotional aspect of addiction to heroin and other substances is the *rip and run* thrill. Teenagers who do not see themselves as successful or do not see life as meaningful make a world for themselves that is filled with a series of daily purposes and successes.

The actual drug is not the purpose. It is the whole process of finding the stuff, getting the money for it, scoring the hit, and then riding the high. They are not

Counselors can help teens find a way out of the misery of drug addiction.

taking drugs, but *doing* drugs. Their day is a whole series of small, yet significant successes.

This false sense of purpose and accomplishment often replaces a teenager's view that life lacks real purpose and accomplishment.

Everyone can find some meaning and purpose in life. They can do so by searching deep within themselves and by setting and working toward goals. Choosing the escape of drugs leads only to a slow process of self- destruction. Repeated use of heroin or any chemical substance corrodes the brain, the organs, and the body. This path is a sure journey to death. Searching within and acting upon your values and goals is a road to life.

Running away from home makes many teenagers easy prey for drug pushers and pimps.

CHAPTER 3

The Start of an Addiction

*H*eroin is not very difficult to get. Most people, like Michael and Jason, get it from their friends. Others get it off the streets.

Major drug dealers often try to work through a network of high school students. This way they are in less danger of getting caught and also have better access to possible buyers. These outside dealers are usually the gangs and pushers who smuggle the drug into the country. The usual addict never meets these people. The addict gets his drugs from his friends who deal.

An addiction begins in experimentation. Someone hears a lot about a drug and decides to experience it for himself. However, heroin is so amazingly addictive that even experimenting with it just a few times can get you hooked.

27

28 Theo was already heavily into pot and acid when he first tried heroin. He'd tried cocaine before, but hadn't liked it. It made him too jumpy and paranoid. Heroin seemed just the thing. It chilled him out, made him feel good.

Soon Theo was using all the time. He never went to class; he just hung around school dealing to support his addiction. Before he'd started using, Theo had had lots of girls after him. But now he'd gone from looking like a healthy, attractive teenager to looking like a corpse. He'd lost his appetite, and when he did eat he became so badly constipated that it was hardly worth the effort. He rarely slept. Track marks ran all up his arms. His eyes were dull and always spaced out. He hardly ever showered. He was a mess.

Theo's parents finally got sick of their son's drug problem. He packed a bag and split.

Theo lived here and there—with friends for as long as they would put up with him, on the streets when he had nowhere else to go. Dealing no longer supported his habit, so he started stealing money, breaking into houses, and prostituting himself. He looked so bad that he barely made enough money selling himself to

When you buy heroin on the street you could be buying anything.

support his habit, which now cost more than $50 a day.

Theo needed more and more heroin to get high. His normal dose would have killed a first-time user. His body had built up a tolerance to the drug. It was only a matter of time before Theo overdosed.

Friends who give or sell you drugs are just like any other dealer. They are not doing you a favor or trying to put excitement into your life. Most likely, they are dealing in order to support their own habit. They "do" the profit. For example, they buy an eighth of an ounce packet, called an *eight ball*. They take some of it for themselves, and then *step on it*, that is, add any white powder, such as baking soda or cornstarch, to bring the weight up. They then resell it as an eight ball. When you buy heroin, you can never know what else you're getting with it.

Sometimes users mix cocaine and heroin together and smoke the mixture. This is incredibly dangerous. A mixture such as this killed actor River Phoenix. He died of a heart attack. His system couldn't take that amount of drugs.

Heroin is a dangerous drug. It became a serious problem among young people in the late 1960s, so much so that it was the leading cause of death for young men in New York City.

Drug dealers know that most people begin using through friends. They offer free hits to students whom they consider possible runners until the targets are hooked. Then when they have to start buying their own stuff, the dealer tells them to sell some and take their share from the profits.

Some dealers offer female students free heroin until they get hooked. The girls are then forced to prostitute themselves for their supply. The dealers usually use the girls themselves at first. When they tire of the girls they start them on a career in the streets.

Through this process, the dealers insure that they have a market and a network in which to move the market. Most gang members do not use drugs themselves. They see the results and don't want to destroy themselves. All they want is profit. They have no concern for you personally. All you are to them is supply and demand.

Family

Unfortunately, many young people get drugs from family members. They often believe that they can trust such a supply. That is false security. The family member has to purchase the stuff from the same dealers the students at school do. It may not be the same person, but the heroin has traveled through the same unsavory channels.

The fact that heroin is illegal in this country and is not even allowed for medical purposes doubles its danger. Using even the cleanest heroin destroys your body, but unmeasured, unclean heroin can do so faster.

When parents drink and smoke, the stage is set for their teenagers to experiment with drugs.

CHAPTER 4

Why?

*T*here are many reasons people begin using drugs. No matter how reasonable
they sound, there is no excuse for doing
drugs.

Family
The largest population of substance
abusers is the adult community. There-
fore it should not surprise us to learn
that most teenagers are taught to do drugs
by their parents.

As children, we learn that the way to
resolve problems is a pill. We see our
parents smoke, drink, maybe even do
heroin themselves. Children naturally
copy their parents. The drugs may not be
the same, but the behavior of taking a
substance to cure, forget, or tolerate a
problem is.

34   Children who grow up in a substance-abusive home are much more likely to become addicts themselves. They learn that taking drugs is normal, is what adults do. When they become adults, they adopt the behavior they have been taught.

Curiosity

Drugs are a great mystery to many teens. They are whispered about everywhere. Movies are made about them, songs are sung about them. Very few teenagers have ever actually been told everything they need to know about drugs.

For some reason, drugs are often regarded by young people, and actually by adults, as glamorous. All kinds of famous people are addicted to drugs or have died from drug use. Even though this should clearly point out the danger of drugs, it tends to have the opposite effect. People wonder what's so great about drugs that makes so many people use them.

There is something very attractive about the darkness and despair associated with heroin. It seems very real, very down to earth. The drug conjures up the image of a tortured artist, using drugs to find inspiration. However, the truth is that heroin will not bring inspiration. It will take over your life until nothing is left but the need for the drug. The attraction of heroin is built on lies. If you want to be an artist, or a writer, or a musician, find your muse elsewhere. Doing heroin will only make you lazy and uninspired.

Peer Pressure

Being a teenager is rough. Pressure comes from everywhere—your family, your school, yourself. Possibly the hardest thing to deal with is pressure from your friends.

If you are doing something that you know is wrong, but you want to keep on doing it, you have an inner conflict. That usually results in guilt. To get rid of that feeling of guilt, it is normal to try to justify your actions.

Students who do drugs often try to talk their friends into doing it because that makes their behavior seem more acceptable. If everyone else is shooting heroin, it must not be so bad a thing after all, right?

Peers who try to pressure you into doing drugs are not doing you a favor. They may be trying to justify their behavior to themselves. They may be trying to get you hooked so they can deal to you and support their own habit. One thing

35

36 is certain. Any friend who is not willing to accept you for who you are and for the choices you make is no friend.

It can be hard to say no to a friend who is pressuring you. But you have to learn to make your own decisions. Your friend isn't living your life, you are. Do what feels right to you. Don't do drugs just because your friend tells you you're not cool if you don't. That friend is wrong.

Pain and Hurt

Heroin resembles morphine, which is sometimes still used today as a painkiller. That is one of the biggest attractions of drugs in general and heroin in particular. They kill the pain of life.

Being a teenager is never easy. Life can be painful. Sometimes people with big problems turn to drugs as an escape.

If you can't cope with your life, if reality is simply too difficult for you, you may see drugs as a relief. Life can be very harsh. You may be suffering from abuse in your family. You may be living in poverty and see no chance of ever escaping. Someone you love dearly may have left you, through rejection or through death. Many things nowadays happen to teenagers that should never happen to anyone.

Living up to your responsibilities helps to create a positive self-image.

38   Heroin makes you feel numb. You forget about the problems that you can't face. You become lost in a kind of dream world. Drugs might seem like the perfect salvation from a life you can't handle.

However, this is one of the nastiest false promises heroin makes. Yes, the high will make you forget about your problems; but when you come down the problems are still there, waiting for you. And after a while you have a whole new problem to deal with: your new heroin addiction.

You can't resolve your problems while you're high. If anything, you're more likely to make them worse. The problems will not go away, and you cannot run from them forever. Getting into heroin just gives you a new set of problems.

Leaving problems unresolved is never a good idea. You have to learn to cope with whatever life throws at you. Using drugs is not a way of coping, it's a way of hiding. It doesn't make you strong enough to deal, it shows you to be too cowardly to stand up to whatever is so horrible.

Your life may be difficult. It may be unbearable. Every person at one time or another feels a sense of need. Every person at some point feels hurt and pain.

In an outpatient rehabilitation center, teenage heroin addicts receive daily doses of methadone as replacement therapy.

We always have freedom to choose how to handle the situation. We can choose to run and hide. We can choose to blame everyone else. We can choose drugs. The point is that it *is* our choice. We can always choose to face life as it is. We can also change it, but only through clear thinking.

There is no situation that we cannot change or survive. No matter how bad the circumstances, there is always somewhere to go, someone who'll help, and some way to climb out of it. Choosing drugs is one way. Choosing life is another.

Many teenagers lose friends to death from heroin overdose.

CHAPTER 5

A Life of Heroin

*H*eroin is not quite as swiftly danger-ous as some people believe. It destroys the body from the inside, slowly but unstoppably. Yet many people do survive for years despite daily use. However, taking heroin regularly is incredibly addictive.

People have remarkably short memo-ries. Just a few years ago, heroin was considered the drug of people who were deeply suicidal. It was said that no one who had any sense would put themselves at the mercy of a drug that was so certainly addictive and so certainly deadly.

Recently, however, heroin has once again come back in fashion. People have

41

forgotten the devastation it can cause. Once again heroin is exerting its evil charm.

Users become addicted to heroin incredibly quickly. Heroin addiction is more severe than even cocaine addiction. It is impossible to stop using without getting professional help.

Recently, heroin has become much more pure than it was just ten years ago. Back then, a fix was usually 4 percent pure heroin—now the average is 65 percent pure. This higher grade of drug allows users to smoke heroin and get extremely high. Many people who were scared away from the drug by fear of needles became addicted by smoking.

What these smokers don't realize is that once you become addicted and your tolerance builds up, smoking will not be able to support your addiction. Almost all users who begin by smoking end up mainlining. Once again, this dark drug has tricked people into addiction.

Addiction to heroin rules your life. You don't think of anything but where to get your next fix. You don't do anything but get high. Nothing is important to you except the drug. Junkies almost never take care of themselves. They often get body

lice, they pay so little attention to
hygiene.

In time you become a slave to the drug. You do not live your life; heroin lives your life. The drug becomes your master, your king, and your god. And eventually your life ends at the whim of that god.

Health

When you choose to do heroin you choose to be sick. It is nearly impossible to stay healthy once you are hooked. The question is how quickly your body is destroyed.

Using heroin brings with it a whole family of health problems. You lose your appetite after a while. You become constipated so that even when you are hungry you don't want to eat. You lose so much weight that you look like a skeleton and usually suffer from severe malnutrition. You no longer take care of your physical appearance, and don't bother to be clean. You have needle tracks on your arms or on your legs, depending on where you shoot up. You have *abscesses*, where your skin caves in making an indentation where you missed a vein while shooting up. You may contract blood diseases from sharing needles, such as hepatitis,

44 endocarditis, septicemia, and perhaps even **AIDS**. You won't be able to stay awake for any length of time. When you crash from a high, you will have horrible stomach cramps, sweats, and chills.

Then there is the danger of overdosing. Every time you get high there comes a point when you crave more heroin, you want to get even higher. That is one reason so many people overdose. When you reach this point, you are too high to realize that you are about to give yourself a fatal dose. Also, as your tolerance grows, you begin to need more heroin to feel anything. Your addiction gets to the point where every fix is enough heroin to kill you. And eventually, it does.

Have you ever seen someone overdosing? It is frightening. The user begins to have convulsions so strong that he or she travels across the room jerking and gyrating. He or she loses control of bodily functions—mucus pours out of the eyes and nose; the person drools or vomits, and may drown in the vomit; he or she may urinate or defecate all over himself. He or she may go into a coma for weeks, months, or years, or may never come out of it. The person may not die; he or she may only have permanent brain damage.

A heroin addict presents an attractive picture, don't you think?

45

Emotions
If you start doing heroin to feel better, you are in for a big disappointment. Part

Loneliness and depression are frequent companions of drug addicts.

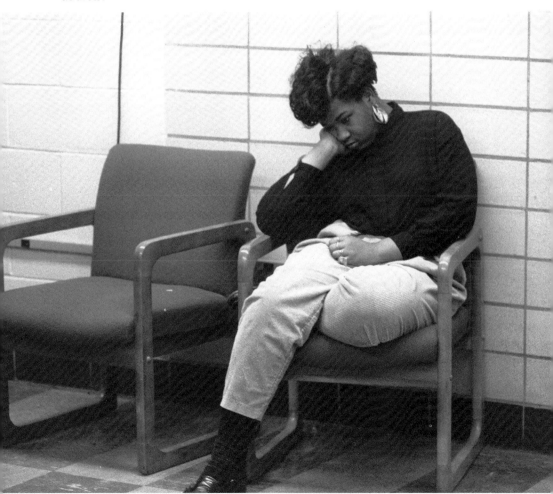

46 of addiction is psychological dependency. It leads to depression and often to suicide. Addicts are sometimes forced into prostitution, dealing, and murder. They have no respect for themselves. Finally, they recognize their dependence on the drug and hate themselves for it. But still they won't stop. They are slaves to heroin, and there is no emotional pain worth that.

Law

Heroin is an illegal narcotic. Trafficking, sale, even possession is a felony crime. Felony crimes mean time in prison.

First-time offenders caught using heroin for reasons not connected to any other crimes may be offered a diversion program. In such a program some states give teenagers the option of volunteering at their own expense to get counseling, drug prevention education, and periodic urinalysis. If they complete this program successfully, the charges can be dropped. Not all states have this option, nor do you have the choice on your second offense. In such cases you are charged as a criminal.

Another danger facing the user is that once you are arrested, or *popped*, you may no longer be trusted by your junkie friends. They may think you are now **47** working with the police. You may not be able to score a hit for a while after your arrest.

If someone is afraid you might *narc*, or inform to the police, he may give you a *hot shot*. This is an overdose of heroin laced with some kind of poison. It will kill you. Dealers sometimes give hot shots to people they don't trust, or even just to junkies who owe them money.

Death

No matter which route you take when you do heroin, you always wind up at the same destination. If you don't get help, you will die. It's that simple.

Don't get yourself into that situation. Don't start doing heroin. You are too valuable a human being to let heroin control and end your life.

Positive activities with positive people are a good defense against the temptation to do drugs.

CHAPTER 6

How to Get Help

*I*t is important to remember that no situation is ever hopeless. Many people who take drugs may find that hard to believe. You may think your condition is worse than it really is. Don't forget that heroin changes your brain.

Addiction is difficult, but *withdrawal is possible.* Habits are hard to break, but *behavior can be changed.* Sickness is hard to overcome, but *people are healed.*

What to Do First

The first step toward help is admitting that you have a problem. The next step is to be willing to take action. The third step is to find help. The final step is to commit yourself to the path to recovery.

The first two steps involve you. You make your own choices about your quality of life. It may seem that you are trapped in your life, but that is simply not so. You decide how you react to your situation. No one can control your thoughts or your wishes.

No one can force you to take drugs. No one can force you not to. Maybe incidents of control do occur. For example, if you are in a hospital or in jail you may not be able to shoot up on heroin. If you are enslaved or captured by a gang, you may be forced to take drugs. But look back on your actions. Your own choice of behavior put you in those situations.

If you have allowed circumstances to open you to addiction to heroin, you can still choose to get out. Once you face the need and decide to withdraw, there are many places to go for help.

Family, Friends, Religious Groups

The first place to go is to your family. Most drug addiction involves the whole family, either directly or indirectly. If other members of your family are involved

in substance abuse, including alcohol, they *51*
will need help as much as you do.

Maybe they don't take part in substance
abuse. But if they create problems for you
through physical or psychological abuse or
neglect or misunderstandings, group
therapy can help you solve your differ-
ences. If your family relationship is
healthy, you will need the love and support
of family members to pull you through the
ordeal.

Sometimes teenagers do not want their
family to know they are involved in drugs.
There are other choices. Other relatives or
close friends can help you. School counselors can suggest help. Family doctors
will treat you or refer you to someone who
specializes in substance abuse. Many
communities offer social services that
include teen centers.

One of the best sources of help is a
religious organization. Most of the people
in such organizations are trained in counseling and have access to community services. For example, Phoenix, Arizona, has
an organization called Clergy Against
Drugs. These inner-city pastors are
trained in assisting young people who
want to withdraw from heroin or other
substances. Most large cities have Jewish

Family Services, listed in the telephone book as a resource for those of the Jewish faith.

Rapha is a national organization that offers in-hospital or outpatient care for substance abusers (1-800-227-2547).

Teen Challenge has offices in big cities.

Heroin is a powerful addiction. Finding professional help is the next step.

Help Is a Phone Call Away

Whether your family is in on your decision or you are struggling alone, you will need trained assistance in withdrawing from heroin. Call a local hotline to find what is available in your area and which programs you can afford or qualify for.

Every major television network announces statewide hotline numbers to call for help. They usually follow a "Say No to Drugs" announcement.

The telephone book has listings in the Yellow Pages. Look in the "D" listings for *Drug Abuse Information and Treatment*. Call one of the clinics or centers and tell them what you need. If one is not the right place for you, they can refer you to other numbers.

If there are no drug listings in your area, try the "A" listings for *Alcoholism*.

You can get help without giving your name on an emergency hotline.

These centers work with the drug abuse centers.

The advantage of phoning for information is that you can be helped to some degree without giving any personal information. The volunteer can tell you which

53

54 clinics will treat you confidentially. Also, clinics range from free to over $2,000 per week in cost. Phoning can help you find the place you can afford. Always remember that help is just a phone call away.

Hotline Emergency

The inside cover of the phone book lists emergency hotlines. They usually have the words *drug, emotional, help,* or *hope* in the number. For example, the number in New York is 1-800-622 HELP for the National Institute on Drug Abuse Treatment Referral. In Arizona the number 1-800-475 HOPE is advertised on television. These are important to know if you are with an overdose victim. Call 911 or one of the emergency numbers.

Some states have emergency teams that specialize in overdoses. Arizona has an organization called TERROS. These men and women rush to the scene in plain clothes and treat the victim without involving the police. That can be an important consideration. The sight of uniforms or the sound of sirens can frighten an overdose victim into a heart attack.

Guidance 55

Every major metropolitan area and most counties have services for withdrawal from drugs. They range from government-funded projects to private hospitals. Religious organizations also provide counseling services.

Remember that substance abuse usually involves hidden causes. If you have been using heroin for any length of time, you will need to repair your thinking as well as heal your body. Good counseling and a relationship with a care group will help you to stay off the drug.

Kicking the habit will also mean changing some of your social habits. You might want to consider a new set of friends. Hanging around friends who are into drugs will be too great a temptation.

Treatment centers can introduce you to new friends who will understand what you are going through and can help you.

Treatment and Rehab Centers

Since withdrawal from heroin "cold turkey" can be painful, many are afraid to quit. That does not have to be the case.

56 Treatment centers offer controlled withdrawal with the help of other substances such as methadone and maltrexone. Some clinics employ acupuncture.

Such treatment enables a person to come off the drug slowly. It also allows him to function at work or school in a normal routine. Withdrawal does not have to be painful.

Unfortunately, many states do not offer methadone to teenagers unless they have failed one or two 21-day detoxification programs.

The programs for teenagers that have been most successful are the rehabilitation centers where they live with other teens coming off the drug.

Helping others is the best way to help yourself. The advantage of living with other addicts is that you can share experiences. There is someone who understands what you are going through.

Rehabilitation centers offer drug abusers a chance to take themselves away from their old environment in a setting that is drug-free. Through counseling and group therapy, they learn ways to rebuild their lives so that they can be free of dependence on heroin or other drugs.

Alcoholic Anonymous and Narcotics Anonymous achieve their success rates by helping their members renew their relationship with family and God. If you belong to a religious organization, or even if you go to a new one where your past is not known, you will be strengthened.

So much of the battle with substance abuse is an inner struggle. Much of the appeal of any drug is emotional and mental. You want peace, freedom from stress, and a sense of well-being.

These can be found on a permanent basis, but not through drugs. Get in touch with your inner self, and strength will come to help you battle the temptation offered by drugs. Find a true and spiritual relationship, and you will find peace, security, well-being, and love.

57

Glossary
Explaining New Words

addiction Inability to resist the urge for a drug.

alternative Choice between two or more courses of action.

cold turkey Quitting the use of a drug without any help.

comatose State of being unconscious, caused by disease, injury, or poison.

constipation Difficult passage of hard, dry feces.

corrosive Gradually eating away, like rust.

cut To mix heroin with a powder.

derivative Made from another material.

eight ball Eighth of an ounce packet.

emulate To try to be like someone.

felony Serious crime that results in severe punishment.

hot shot Overdose of heroin, or a dose laced with poison designed to kill the user.

injection Placing of a substance directly
into the blood, usually with a needle.

junkie Person addicted to drugs.

laboratory Place where scientists work.

mainline To inject heroin directly into the
blood through a vein.

malnutrition Poor health caused by not
eating an adequate diet.

popped Arrested.

prosecute To charge in court with a
crime.

prostitute Person who is paid for per-
forming sexual acts.

rehabilitation Restoring to former
health, or putting back into good condition.

rig The needle and tourniquet used to
inject heroin.

rip and run Process of doing drugs in
which you *rip* or get the drug and then
run to find more.

scoring a hit Buying heroin.

shooting gallery Place where people
gather to get shots of heroin.

skin pop To inject heroin under the skin,
not directly into the vein.

step on it Slang term for taking some
heroin out of a packet and adding back
some kind of powder to make the
packet look full again.

Help List

- American Council for Drug Education
  204 Monroe Street
  Rockville, MD 20852
  (301) 294-0600

- National Clearinghouse for Alcohol and
    Drug Information
  P.O Box 2345
  Rockville, MD 20852
  (301) 468-2600

- Narcotics Anonymous
  World Service Office
  16155 Wyandotte Street
  Van Nuys, CA 91406

- National Federation of Parents for
    Drug-Free Youth
  8730 Georgia Avenue
  Silver Spring, MD 20910
  1-800-554-KIDS (5437)

- NIDA Clearinghouse for Drug
    Information
  P.O Box 416

Kensington, MD 20795

For Further Reading

Ball, Jacqueline. *Everything You Need to Know about Drug Abuse*, rev. ed. New York: Rosen Publishing Group, 1994.

Godfrey, Martin. *Heroin*. New York: Franklin Watts, 1987.

Kaplan, Leslie. *Coping with Peer Pressure*, rev.ed. New York: Rosen Publishing Group, 1994.

Lee, Essie E. *Breaking the Connection*. New York: Julian Messner, 1988.

62 Morgan, H. Wayne. *Drugs in America.* New York: Syracuse University Press, 1981.

Smith, Sandra Lee. *Coping with Decision-Making.* New York: Rosen Publishing Group, 1989.

_____. *Coping through Self-Control.* New York: Rosen Publishing Group, 1991.

Sunshine, Linda; Wright, John. *The 100 Best Treatment Centers for Alcoholism and Drug Abuse.* New York: Avon Books, 1988.

Toma, David; Levey, Irv. *Toma Tells It Straight with Love.* New York: Bantam, Doubleday, Dell, 1981.

U.S. Department of Justice. *Drugs of Abuse.* Washington, D.C.: Drug Enforcement Agency, 1992.

Index

About the Author

Sandra Lee Smith has taught grades from kindergarten through college in California and Arizona.

In response to the President's Report, *A Nation at Risk*, Ms. Smith participated in a project involving Arizona State University, Phoenix Elementary School District, and an inner-city community in Phoenix. Participants in the project developed a holistic approach to education.

Photo Credits

Cover Photo: Chuck Peterson
Photos on pages 2, 9, 25, 29, 32, 37, 40, 45, 48, 59: Chris Volpe; page 13: Gamma-Liaison/Dr. Allan W. King; page 17: Gamma-Liaison/Roger M. Richards; page 20: Chuck Peterson/Blackbirch Graphics; page 26: Gamma-Liaison/James Metropole, page 39: Wide World.

Design/Production: Blackbirch Graphics, Inc.